DEMAIN PUE

C000148686

Short Sharp Shocks!

Murder! Mystery! Mayhem!

Beats! Ballads! Blank Verse!

Weird! Wonderful! Other Worlds

Horror Novels & Novellas

Science Fiction Novels & Novellas

The 'A QUIET APOCALYPSE' Series

General Fiction

Science Fiction Collections

Horror Fiction Collections

Anthologies

Audios

NEVER REACHING THE END

BY
PAULA R.C. READMAN

COPYRIGHT INFORMATION

For further information, please visit:
WEB: www.demainpublishing.com
TWITTER: @DemainPubUk
FACEBOOK: Demain Publishing
INSTAGRAM: demainpublishing

ACKNOWLEDGEMENTS

A big thank you goes to my dear neighbours, Dave and Joan Richardson for being my inspiration when I wrote *The Funeral Birds*, and for your continuing support and laughter. Also, a big thanks goes to my husband, Russell for his time, patience and hard work. He's my rock, moon, and stars, the wonderful guy who pays the bills. Hopefully, if the Saint of Struggling Authors is looking down upon me, he will sprinkle some gold dust, and I'll be able to reward you with a shiny new car.

To my little sister, Gwynneth and her husband, John, I'm so pleased that the stars have realigned themselves once more, giving us this opportunity to get to understand each other better. The world looks so much brighter.

Once again, my heart-warming thanks to DEMAIN Publishing and Dean M. Drinkel for accepting another submission from me. Granny Wenlock and I are busy writing another submission as this twisted tale, *Never Reaching the End* goes into print.

And, to everyone else who knows me, please buy my books, enjoy them and leave a review, or else you might find yourself between the covers of the next one, and your ending might not be pleasant.

CONTENTS

CHAPTER ONE

"I love it, Blake." Wendy giggled as she spun around, arms outstretched in the centre of the dusty room. "It feels like home."

"You're making me dizzy," I said, laughing with her. I had forgotten the sound of her laughter. It verged on childlike in its sweetness, never seeming false when she was happy. I could almost believe our dark days were behind us. Why she found the abandoned house so desirable was beyond me. Signs of dilapidation ate into every part of the building. The walls showed signs of dampness as stained wallpaper clung in desperation as though trying to defeat gravity. Broken glass in the windows allowed the rain in, which permitted rot and fungi to eat into the wooden frames. Was nature reclaiming the abode for itself? The smell tore at my throat.

Was it mildew or something else?

I moved towards the window, hoping the fresh air would help. In every corner, intricate cobwebs dangled like long-forgotten Christmas garlands swaying lightly in a draft. They crossed the room connecting the light fittings to the peeling wallpaper. Fragments of the ceiling plaster littered the dusty floorboards among the skeletal leaves. The only signs of recent tenants were rodents and bird droppings that littered the surfaces, along with corpses of flies, moths, a dead rat, and what appeared to be a dead squirrel in one of the corners.

Soft sunlight leached between the slats that boarded up the windows, creating a spotlight on Wendy as she spun around. In a whirlwind of dust particles, she seemed almost ethereal in appearance. Her dark brown hair shone as it lifted from her shoulders. If the place hadn't been so grubby, I would've reached out and pulled her into my embrace. I wanted so much to taste the sweetness of her kisses, to lose myself in the depth of her sparkling eyes, and to feel the warmth of her naked body against mine. I knew this would be impossible after the fire took everything from us. For now, I was happy to have her return my smiles and to hear her laughter.

*

Four years ago, Wendy had planned her first evening out since having our children. She had thrown herself into motherhood, sacrificing her social life. After the birth of Alex, I became a person of no importance to my wife, only the idiot who paid the bills. She wouldn't let me near her or the child. Morning, noon, and night, the first words out of her mouth were 'the baby'.

It was short of a bloody miracle when she fell pregnant again. I had no recollection of the intimacy that brought about the birth of Tina.

How had I managed it?

I wondered whether the wolf had snuck in the back door one night while I worked my balls off to keep it from the front. I never questioned Wendy's loyalty. With two young children so close together, along with the housework, I couldn't imagine her finding time to be unfaithful. We were both shattered by the end of the day, with just enough energy to crawl into bed and fall asleep.

*

"We could really make this place our own, Blake," Wendy said coming to an abrupt halt without the slightest wobble in her step. "This room would make a lovely bedroom."

The details the estate agent had given us were almost right, I thought as I glanced through a gap in the boarded-up window. The views of the estuary from the back of the house were amazing on a sunny, winter's day when the trees were bare. In the summer, invisible—

"Are you listening to me, Blake?" Wendy's sharp voice tore through my thoughts.

"Yes, of course." I turned. The joy, which had softened her features in the morning, was gone.

"You don't like the house, do you?" she snarled; her eyes were black slits.

The suffocating dankness, along with the smell, turned my stomach. I took a deep breath, choosing my words carefully. "It's the amount of work needed before we can think about moving in—" I muttered.

Wendy's face told me all I needed to know. Wrong answer.

"The outlook is great. The garden is vast. Do we need so much land?" I quickly added while giving a light laugh to break the growing tension.

"It all comes with the house. We can sell a few hectares or rent it out to help with the cost of repairing the house."

"Who to?"

Wendy gestured across the water at the marina full of yachts and other small boats. "Plenty of boat owners are looking for cheap moorings, so if we make a small investment and build a landing stage along the water's edge. Then people with horses would take care of the jungle out there." Wendy crossed the room and pulled open a cupboard door. It creaked, cutting into the dust on the floor. "Once the house is ours, let's make a list–oh, how odd." She said, peering into the cupboard.

"What's wrong?" I crossed to her side.

"It's not a cupboard...but another room." Wendy switched on her phone and lit up the darkness before stepping in. "We could turn it into a dressing room or maybe an ensuite."

"Maybe." I flicked through the other property details we had planned to view. The other houses were in far better condition and less strain on our limited funds. I hadn't been keen on the house from the start, it unnerved me.

CHAPTER TWO

Two hours earlier, our satnav had us bumping along an unmade road; we believed a service company used to maintain the twin mobile phone towers just visible between the trees. A high brick wall edged one side of the road. Suddenly, the satnav barked, 'Your destination is on your right.'

We had reached a kind of crossroads. One side continued towards the towers, and on the other stood a mass of weeds, shrubs, and ivy while the wall continued off into the distance. Wendy stopped before an oak tree. Its massive branches blocked out the bright sunshine.

"Where do we turn for the house?" I asked, climbing out to have a look around. "Are you sure we're at the right place?"

"Yes, we're here." Wendy studied her phone. A puzzled look settled on her face as she rubbed her forehead before glancing around as though trying to compare the map on her phone to reality. I walked to the oak tree and began studying the surroundings. Why had the satnav brought us to this spot?

There wasn't anything other than overgrown shrubs, weeds, and tumbling ivy. I put my hand out and leaned against the tree trunk. A strange sensation engulfed me as I felt the roughness of the bark beneath my fingertips. The landscape had changed. It appeared free from dead weeds, the tangle of brambles, ivy, and shrubs. Beyond the tree stood a wall of bright red bricks and a pair of black and gold ornate gates. The freshly cut grass added to an air of newness, which radiated around me. A plaque set high on the wall glinted in the dappled sunlight.

"Ravenglass Hall," I muttered. The estate agent had called it Estuary Hall, Thimble Island, on their website.

A sudden flash of sunlight blinded me. When I looked again, the tangle of dead weeds, bramble and ivy had returned. Had I seen a gap in the wall? Maybe, the branches moving in the breeze caused a trick of the light. I moved forward, crushing the tall thistles and nettles with my boots. I reached the spot where I thought I had seen the gates and tugged the ivy aside. To my astonishment, some ironwork appeared.

"Hey, there's a gap in the wall here, with gates," I said. "It must have been a while ago, when the estate agents came to photograph the place."

"The house has been on the market quite a while, Blake. That's why we can afford it. Are there padlocks on the gates? If there are, we'll have to look for another way in. According to Google Maps, there's no other entrance on this side."

"Your luck's in," I said, tugging another large piece of ivy away. I smiled over my shoulder. To my surprise and delight, Wendy returned it. My heart lifted. Did this mean we had reached a turning point since the tragedy? I tore at the ivy with renewed vigour. On clearing one of the gates, with a bit of a struggle, I managed to pull it open. Wendy, with care, manoeuvred the car through. I closed the gate behind us, which seemed a little stupid, but I didn't care.

The long winding drive, cleared at some point, going by the stumps and pitting in its surface, was now suffering from growback over the past seasons. As Wendy swerved around stumps and dodged potholes, the house slowly revealed only the tops of its towers above the tree tops until we turned the final corner.

The gothic house with its towers, turrets, and dormer windows rose from the ground like a living thing and fitted perfectly in with its surroundings of long-lived trees and the estuary glinting in the sunshine beyond it. The calls of geese and wildfowl overhead made me shiver as unfamiliar thoughts crowded my mind. Wendy was out of the car in a flash and stood hugging herself. Her face radiated her joy and excitement.

"Oh, Blake, it's wonderful. It looks more beautiful than I thought possible."

Did my wife see the building in the same light as me? Windows boarded up, while others were broken. Tiles were missing from parts of the roof, while ivy worked its way around one of the towers and, no doubt, under the roof, too. Everything looked broken, including the stone steps leading to an ornate, covered brick porch. The house was in desperate need of specialist renovations to make it liveable. I took a deep breath and trailed after Wendy as she circled the house. It seemed too secure to get in, much to Wendy's disgust. Over breakfast at her parents' home, she decided it would be better to view the property; without going through the estate agent. "We'll look less keen," she had said.

She was right, of course. We didn't have the money to look too keen. If the property needed a lot of work, we could get the price reduced with prior knowledge. The insurance payout from our old home would barely cover the cost of fixing the roof, I thought as Wendy tugged at a panel covering a door at the back of the building. Going by the state of the house, even if the seller offered it to us free, I still felt the cheapest option would be to build a new one on the site, with all mod-cons.

"Come on, Blake, stop daydreaming, and help." Wendy had pulled a screwdriver from her pocket and was trying to jemmy the panel free from the doorway.

"Not a good idea to enter the building. It looks dangerous."

"Help me, Blake. You can stay out here, but I'm going in!"

I took the screwdriver from her and began unscrewing the panel. When the screwdriver made contact with the screw head a tingling sensation raced through my arm, causing my fingers to clench. The unbearable pain, like red-hot needles, punched my palm while in my head; a low echoing cry filled my mind. The pain behind the crying was not my own but someone else's.

"We'll be here all day at this rate!" Wendy said, her voice full of bitterness. "Pull it off!"

"Stand back then." I picked up a large branch and snapped off some of its smaller ones. I tested its strength before jamming the thickest part under the panel. To help me get some leverage, I looked around for a brick.

"What are you doing?"

"Trying to make it easier for myself."

"Get on with it."

Mustering as much force as I could, I pushed hard down on the branch. The panel seemed almost to pop off as though there was some internal force at work. A cracking noise echoed around us, causing a flock of noisy crows to take flight, followed by a rushing sound as though the house was exhaling after holding its breath for too long. A cloud passed over the sun, causing a shadow to race across the ground. I looked up, lifting my hand to shield my eyes. The glass in every window shone as the beauty of the building revealed itself to me. I gasped and gripped my chest in fear.

"For God's sake Blake, let me pass." Wendy dragged the panel from the entrance. Then with no hesitation, after rubbing the dirt from her hands, she stepped into the darkness of the building. I lingered outside as an overwhelming feeling of dread took hold of me. To waste time, I returned the branch and the brick from where I had taken them. As I placed the brick on the crumbling garden wall, someone spoke. Their voice sounded intimate, as though they expected to find me waiting there.

"Oh, there you are, Blake."

On straightening, I turned, pleased that Wendy's good humour had returned, but no one was there.

CHAPTER THREE

"About what?" I looked up; my thoughts interrupted while studying the printouts.

"An ensuite. Would be ideal, don't you think?"

"It smells like something died in there." I leaned against the doorframe.

"Well, I don't smell anything." Wendy panned around with her phone, caught in its beam some dark staining on the bare plaster walls along with what looked to be deep scratch marks.

"There's a small boarded-up window here," she said, pointing to the back wall. "We'll be able to enlarge it. If the bath was here." Wendy drew a line with the toe of her shoe on the dusty floor. "The view from it would be amazing as you lay in the bath. It must be a Victorian one with claw feet."

"Wendy, it's an old house. There's bound to be planning restrictions."

"It's worth taking a risk, don't you think?" she said brightly, making her way towards me.

"My honest opinion, Wendy, It's a gamble. A bottomless pit. We shouldn't have broken in."

"Does it really matter?" she shrugged. "It's better than having an estate agent trailing after us."

"Yes, I suppose you're right, but—at least we could've found out more about the property."

"Like what?"

"Important stuff—like whether there are any restrictions on what we can do, and if it is a listed building, does it mean there's a restriction on who can carry out the work? It might be the reason it is still on the market. The land is expensive around here, especially with so much water frontage. Wendy, we should look at the other properties before settling on this one."

Even by the light of her phone, I saw her eyes flare as her brow furrowed. "I want this house," she snarled.

"For Christ's sake, look around you." I waved the property details at her while trying to keep my voice even. "Let's crunch a few numbers. Get some idea of the cost of the renovations."

She pushed me. No, more like shoved me, out of the way. Her footsteps echoed her anger back at me as she hurried along the landing. As I reached for the cupboard door, the smell of decay engulfed me. I dropped to my knees, gagging. I tried to draw in deep breaths, but the odour caught at the back of my throat. Out of the corner of my eye, a glint of silver flashed, followed by a whoosh. The sound filled the dark space. A sheering pain cut across my cheek. Instinctively, my hand flew to my cheek, expecting to feel the warmth of blood or damaged flesh.

Nothing.

Then a voice began a low rhythmic chant, words I couldn't understand. A wave of cold washed over me as my chest restricted. A woman screamed. Once again, I felt Wendy's fists beating my chest as the overpowering smell of smoke made me heave. As my breathing eased, I lifted my head. The back of the door came into view. Deep gouges marked the wood. Knife marks, I thought as I reached out, running my fingertips over them. Had someone been trying to escape the room? I used the door handle to haul myself up, and in the process, I snagged my fingers on the rough surface. I dropped the property printouts and tried to extract the splinter buried along the edge of my nail. I clenched my teeth to fight nausea as I pulled the splinter out. A burning pain raced up my arm. It felt as though I was tearing my arm from its socket. A voice screamed at me as the room swirled in a maelstrom of flashing blues and orange lights.

CHAPTER FOUR

The horrors of four years ago came flooding back. I stood staring in disbelief; on a muddy front lawn at the blazing, dancing lights and mayhem. I was rooted to the spot, choking on the smell of death, unable to tear myself away, even though the heat scorched my skin and the acrid fumes stung my eyes.

"Where the bloody hell were you, Blake?" Wendy screamed in my face breaking the spell. "You murdered our children, you bastard!"

"Murdered. What are you saying?"

"They—are—dead—because of you!" she yelled, while pummelling my chest, with her blackened fists, her words made no sense to me.

"They are dead because of you!"

How was it possible? I refused to believe her vile words; I had been at work all day.

As the police officers forced the gawking, videoing, onlookers back onto the footpath. Two fire fighters materialised in the doorway of the smoking building, their breathing-apparatus echoing their deep breaths. They carried a wrapped bundle each. An audible gasp floated up from the onlookers to join the cacophony that filled the once peaceful cul-de-sac. As the fire fighters carefully set the bundles down, I stared in disbelief, recognising the duvets straightaway as my daughters' bedding. I rushed forward and dropped to my knees. The muddy water soaked into my trousers as I pulled and tugged at the bundles. With unexpected ease, the cloth revealed the true horror of the fire as I stared at the blackened dolls with melted faces.

"These are not my beautiful girls!" I whispered into the night that stunk of damp ash and burnt meat. Wendy's screams filled the air as she came up behind me. I leapt to my feet, wanting to take her into my arms and comfort her, but instead held her at arm's length and gazed into her swollen red eyes. Within them, hatred bubbled, a mixture of betrayal, lies, and loathing. They weren't Wendy's eyes, I saw, but Caroline's.

Was I to blame?

I would've been home not long after replying to Wendy's text, asking if I had already left work. *Yes*, I messaged back, but then, Caroline waylaid me in the lift.

*

Oh, the beauty that was Caroline. She was far too available and too willing to make such a fool of me. She was every hot-blooded male's wet dream. Tall, leggy, and slim, with glossy, auburn locks that cascaded around her shoulders, high cheekbones, and come-to-bed eyes. She moved with grace and elegance on stiletto heels, matching their colour to that of her lipstick. Her clothes hugged her curves as though she sought dominance over every male in the office. Caroline had been sniffing around me for ages. On more than one occasion, she had cornered me in the lift, though the clicking of her stilettos warned me of her approach. Sometimes, the early warning of her arrival was the cheap, flowery perfume she wore. The other married men in the office had offered their advice, telling me not to risk my happiness, but I soon learnt their advice wasn't something they had taken themselves.

"She's a vampire. Avoid looking too deeply into her hazel eyes if you do; you're a dead man walking," Sean had said.

He should know. Caroline had gobbled him up and spat him out all within a week. Like most of the men she ensnared, they came with a wedding ring. Commitment wasn't one of her fortes. It seemed to me she couldn't care less about her reputation. I wondered whether she had to prove to herself; no man could resist her charms, or maybe it was simply a case of someone in her past breaking her heart. Now she had nothing more to lose but everything to gain by inflicting her suffering on others.

Such a poor excuse, I know, to say I should've known better, but I needed some light relief. I wasn't looking for a week, not even a day. Just a quick fuck and home before Wendy was due to go out. One minute we were in the lift. The next, in her vehicle, parked a few streets away fucking.

As for some light relief, I didn't achieve it, which served me right. Caroline played me, but in reality, she played us all. Male pride told tall tales around the office. I thought others were laughing behind her back, but in reality, she had the last laugh.

On collecting my car, I wore my regret like cheap perfume while my conscience twisted a knot in my gut. Nausea swept over me as I climbed into my car and drove out of the company car park. All I wanted was a shower and to see my beautiful girls. As I stood staring at my burning home, my dead daughters, and my inconsolable wife, I wondered why I had worried so much about the smell of Caroline's cheap perfume and sex. None of that mattered now.

*

The pain from my damaged nail brought me back to the present. I squeezed my finger along the length of the splinter. When enough of it appeared amongst the blood, I nipped its end with my teeth. The air in the room shifted as I drew it out. A pain tore up my arm, causing my gut to clench. I spat the splinter out and sucked on my bloody finger before wiping it on my jeans. My damaged nail was turning black while the edges looked red-raw.

"No way in heaven or hell," I yelled, slamming the door, "am I going to live here!"

At the top of the stairs, the house seemed to breathe me in. It was too quiet inside as if the whistling wind outside couldn't enter. "This is madness," I shouted while entering another room. "It's too damn big for just the two of us, Wendy!"

There were more signs of decay. Stained walls and fallen ceiling plaster scattered across the floor like drifting snow. There were mice droppings, leaves, and collections of skeletons, the remains of a menagerie visible among the dust, too. The decay seemed to eat its way into me as my chest tightened and a feeling of clamminess washed over me. I rubbed my

throbbing shoulder while my mind drifted back
to the loss of my old home.

*

An hour before the fire swept through my home
Caroline drove me away from the office block
where we worked. My excitement was tangible.
I prayed like never before that the hardness
against my thigh would remain long enough to
enjoy the pleasure Caroline offered me. I had
no idea where she was taking me, and
imagined we were heading towards her luxury
apartment, or maybe one of the nearby high-
class hotels.

A light laugh escaped her lips as she
turned off the main road into a back alley. The
alleyway between the office blocks and the
main high street was full of rubbish and
industrial wheelie bins. Shocked, I turned to
her, unsure whether she had made a mistake
or knew it to be a shortcut, but I had seen a
no-through sign. As Caroline slowed, my ardour
began to sink. I became a nervous teenager on
a first date as Caroline reversed her luxury
Range Rover between two industrial bins and
killed the engine.

The air in the spacious vehicle had
become stifling and sickly sweet with Caroline's
perfume. The only sounds were the drone of
distant traffic and Caroline's heavy breathing. I
closed my eyes and let my breath out slowly,
trying to focus on why I was there.

"Blake, my darling," Caroline twisted in
her seat. "You look utterly scared. Nothing to
worry about, no one can see us here." She said
with her hand on my knee as her long red nails

dug into my flesh. To stop myself flinching, I tried to think of something witty to say, "Do you bring all your dates here or just the special ones?"

"What makes you think you're so special, Blake?" Caroline leaned towards me; her minty breath made my gut constrict. She slid her hand up my leg until it rested on my groin. My breath caught as Caroline gently squeezed me. She released her hair, letting it tumble around her shoulders. I reached out with trembling fingers and unfastened the buttons of her satin blouse. Caroline's breathing steadied to short, even, breaths. As my body reacted to her fondling, I shifted uncomfortably in my seat; my clothes restricted my cock's freedom. On seeing my distress, Caroline unzipped my trousers, leaned forward, and for a fleeting moment, I thought she was going to take me in her mouth, but instead, she kissed my abdomen. Caroline ran her tongue up to my chest as she unbuttoned my shirt. Her excitement bubbled over as she slipped it off my shoulders.

"What a perfect body, Blake. Oh, such a pity about that!" Caroline pointed her nail at the pale puckered skin, shaped like a fifty pence piece, just below the collarbone on my right shoulder.

"Oh, that. It's nothing, just a birthmark." I laughed and leaned in to kiss her, but she shoved me back while her hand released the seat. I shot back and found myself lying almost flat.

In one swift movement, Caroline folded the centre console, climbed over and squatted between my legs. With a glint in her hazel eyes and a naughty smile on her lips, she lowered her head and slipped her hand into my pants.

Excitedly, I lifted my butt, yearning for my cock to be in her mouth, but instead she tugged at my trousers, pulling them down with ease.

Now naked, a wave of vulnerability washed over me as Caroline's beautiful features hardened into a demonic countenance. Her eyes darkened to black slits and locked with mine as she climbed onto me. Her thighs crushed my hips as she rode me.

The pleasure I sought ebbed away, as I fought to close my eyes against the writhing embodiment of evil Caroline had become as she held me trapped between her thighs. The pinkness of her tongue was hypnotic, as it darted between her red lips snake-like, almost tasting the air.

Caroline seemed unaware that her nails were gouging my shoulder as though trying to remove my birthmark. A growing scream bubbled up inside me as I struggled beneath her. The pressure she put on my bladder made me fight her as I tried to take control. She lowered her head to my neck, her mouth a gaping hole lined in blood red. I fought to draw in air as a stinking, sweaty odour filled my lungs making me want to vomit.

My chest reached the point where it felt as though it was about to explode when an unearthly screeching filled my ears. At first, I wasn't sure if it was her or me. It sounded neither passionate nor lustful more like a wounded animal or something possessed. Fear took its toll on me, and my ardour died away.

Caroline sensed the change in me and hissed in my face. "I thought I had met my match in you, Blake, but you're just another weak excuse for a man." She lifted her leg and wiped herself on my shirt before flinging it in my face and climbing back into the driver's seat.

"Take that home to your darling wife. Let her smell the scent of your betrayal. That'll brighten her day. Now get out, you pathetic man." She flung the door open and shoved me, her talons digging into my bare thighs.

In a bid for freedom, I landed unceremoniously on the filthy ground, closely followed by my jacket, as the door banged shut. As Caroline started the engine, I managed to roll clear of the wheels with my trousers still around my ankles. I watched from the side of an overfilled wheelie bin surrounded by the stench of car fumes and takeaways as the red taillights of her vehicle sped away.

After readjusting my clothing, I picked up my jacket from where she had thrown it and slipped it on. Even the reek of fast food couldn't eradicate the stench of Caroline from my nostrils. As I walked back to work to collect my car, I had convinced myself that the fallout of my stupidity was minimal. If my colleagues survived their encounters with Caroline, so could I. When the time was right, I would join *The Brotherhood* beside the water cooler and share in their banter. Caroline would treat me with the same contempt as she treated them, but at least she would no longer sniff around me.

I arrived back at the company car park and was relieved not to encounter anyone. How would I have explained coming back to collect my car? I started the engine and pulled onto the High Street when a wave of guilt washed over me. Indiscretion had a price. To lose my family would destroy me. I laughed at my fears; nothing to worry about apart from a bruised pride and a torn shoulder. I pulled into a service station before heading home. A chilling thought slithered through my mind as I stood leaning against the car, waiting for it to finish charging. *What did any of us know about Caroline? No one seemed to know where she came from, and nothing about her personal life, not even if she had ever been married.*

As I left the city behind, I turned on the music, relaxed in my seat and began practising some excuses for my dishevelled look. "Sorry, had problems with the car. Sorry for arriving home late; Sean needed some help carrying boxes to his car."

CHAPTER FIVE

As a single man, I was a first-rate bastard, even had the t-shirt to prove it. Given time, I could've written a bestselling manual on how to play the field with style. At a party with my latest lay, who had dragged me along, I met Wendy. I can't remember the other girl's name now, though I recalled she was loud, wore short, tight skirts and had ample breasts. She'd gone to find the loo while I fetched some drinks. I found the drinks in the dining room but no clean glasses on the table. I headed for the kitchen, pushed the door open, and came face to face with a domestic goddess elbow-deep in bubbles. My jaw must have hit the floor as our eyes met. I stood gawking, the words dried on my tongue.

The beauty spoke first; her blue eyes cast a spell over me. "Are you looking for someone?"

"Hmm—two clean glasses, please."

"Oh, you'll need to dry them yourself."

I looked around for a tea towel.

"Bottom drawer over there." She pointed a soapy finger.

"Do—do you live here?" I asked, pulling a tea towel out of the drawer, frightened to lose the opportunity of knowing her better. I snatched up a glass and began to dry it slowly.

"No, just got bored of standing around while my friend gets fucked."

"Sorry—what?" My shock must have registered on my face at hearing such language from a delicate mouth.

"No, I'm the one that's sorry. I'm a bit annoyed, please forgive me. My mother would've washed my mouth out with soapy water for using such coarse language. I become a wallflower whenever I get a party invite." The beauty turned back to washing up, adding more plates to the water.

I stared at her profile as she rinsed a plate under the tap before adding it to the drainer. I had finished drying the glasses but couldn't bear the thought of leaving her. I started on the plates. Then she threw me a smile. For the first time in my life, I was contented. All I wanted was to hear this modestly dressed beauty laughing. She wore little makeup, just an air of innocence that had me hooked. I checked her fingers, no ring.

"Would you like a drink?" I asked. She smiled. Such a smile, it lit up her eyes. That did it for me.

"You're the first person to ask me here," she said.

"Don't go anywhere, I'll be back." I dashed from the kitchen, returning with a bottle of wine, forgetting the old girlfriend. "Dry your hands. I'm whisking you away from here."

She laughed, her hair shimmering coppery around her shoulders as she grabbed the wine glasses, I'd just finished drying.

Suddenly caught under Wendy's spell I found a new direction in my life. My unknown past seemed unimportant as I enjoyed planning a new future. I wined and dined Wendy taking the time to get to know her. It made me fall far deeper in love with her than anyone else before.

Three weeks after the party, I met her parents at her insistence. In the past, I would've dumped the girl unceremoniously and gone into hiding, not answering my phone. This time I found myself walking on air. It's a bit of an understatement to say her parents seemed a little more than surprised when I arrived at their door, but as soon as Wendy wrapped her arms around me, pulling me into their hallway, everything seemed so right, and I forgot all about it as she introduced me to them.

CHAPTER SIX

Since the awful day of the fire, all I could do was focus on Wendy's wants and needs. I needed to continue working to pay our way and to keep my sanity. The loss of the children brought everything into sharp focus. As well as blowing a hole in my life, I realised how selfish I had become. For Wendy, the children, the house, and putting meals on the table were all consuming for her, leaving her no time to think about anything else. The reality of being a family meant there wasn't any time left for Wendy and me to be lovers. If I had realised that sooner, I could have been a better husband and father and played my part by focusing on work and paying the bills.

Wendy's parents, Joyce and Roger, suggested I stay with them until their daughter was well enough to leave the hospital. I decided it was the most sensible thing to do. Where else could I have gone?

I had no other family. The couple who fostered me died in a motorway pile-up when I was eighteen. I couldn't bear spending endless lonely nights in a bedsit. It wasn't something I wanted to go through again. Staying with my in-laws gave me a sense of belonging until Wendy was well enough for us to plan a new future together.

Dora and Reg told me about the strange events that led to my fostering when I was old enough to comprehend it. On my eighteenth birthday, Martin my foster brother, and I had packed our camper van for a trip to Wales, a gift from Martin and my foster parents. As we were about to leave, Dora and Reg gave me a photo album of my childhood and a thin folder containing the sparse details of my life, including a newspaper cutting. Dora had collected everything she could about my life before I had arrived in their care. Purely by chance, I'd taken the folder into work on the day of the fire, even though I had copies of everything stored on the Cloud. Over the years, I had read the faded newspaper cutting many times, but still, it made no sense.

Thimble Island Mystery

Yesterday, our local journalist, Douglas Fields was on the scene when two men landed their catch of the day. Douglas asked Peter Robson to explain what happened. Peter had phoned the coastguard to report that they would need an ambulance to meet them at the quayside after they rescued a young child. The coastguard notified the police as the child's parents were missing.

In the early morning, the two men set out to their usual fishing haunt along the creeks off Thimble Island. Peter Robson, the owner of the boat, Cobden, said, "It's all been rather shocking, not something one expects to find. I've been fishing along these creeks for many a year now, and you can haul in the most strange and unexpected things other than fish. I've even taken a refrigerator out and an unforgettable Mini cooper too. If people can move it, they will dump it, but a naked child, I never expected that in all my days. My blood ran cold when I realised he was alive."

When Mr Peter Robson was asked by our journalist how long he thought the boy had been in the water, he said, "It's a hard question to answer as the boy was icy to the touch. I was sure I was pulling a dead body out. Once he was on the deck, he started coughing and gulping. We wrapped him in warm blankets and gave him a hot drink. He shook so much his teeth were chattering. The only word he said was Blake. When I asked him if it was his name, he nodded. After that, he closed his eyes and fell into a deep sleep. The poor lad must have been exhausted, trying to stay afloat in the cold water. When he woke next, he never said another word to me."

Dora and Reg believed that the loss of my parents in such a devastating way wiped my memory. The hospital found nothing physically wrong and thought I had suffered a mental breakdown while struggling to stay afloat in the water. It left me like a new-born trapped in a six-year-old body, unable to speak, walk, or feed myself when they released me into Reg and Dora's care. With their kindness and patience, they nursed me back to health. The police searched the area and found no signs of a sunken boat or wreckage along the shoreline. As time passed, who I was and where I came from remained a mystery.

The whereabouts of my parents concerned my foster parents more than me. They adopted Martin when he was three years old and hoped to give me the same security as they had him. Martin was four years older than I was and took me under his wing. I looked upon him as an older brother.

Of course, I wanted a legal adoption like Martin, so we all had the same surname, but the social services felt until they could establish my identity, I was to remain within the foster system. My surname Cobden came from the name of the boat that belonged to the man who pulled me out of the creek, but Blake was my given name and the only thing I owned from my parents, though it didn't help me in my search for the truth behind their disappearance.

It took months of gentle persuasion from my foster parents for me to talk again, and when I did, I had no memory of my life before the accident. During the first two years of living with my new family, my reoccurring dreams of finding myself trapped kept them awake. Dora began to watch over me. Waking from the nightmare to find I wasn't alone helped me escape them, and in time the dreams faded.

While celebrating my eighteenth birthday in Wales, Martin and I received the tragic news of Reg and Dora's death. We hugged under a starry sky, knowing our perfect life had ended. After the funeral, a solicitor informed us that our foster parents had left us well provided for in their will. Martin and I hugged again for the last time before going our separate ways, and I lost touch with him completely. The devastation was too much for us both, I think. I know it was for me.

The fire triggered the return of my disturbed sleep. On several occasions, I woke bathed in sweat with the taste of the acrid smoke, the hysterical screams of Wendy, and my feeling of helplessness being so vivid. On falling asleep again, the feeling of being crushed returned, followed by trying to stay afloat in the water. Sleep wanted to allow the water to take me, but my need for air was greater as I kept sucking in mouthfuls in my restless dreams.

Sobbing, I tore desperately at the bedcovers that restricted my movements. Once free, I leapt from the bed and dropped to my knees, head in hand, fighting to breathe as my chest constricted. A burning pain tore through my right shoulder. It felt so real I clung to my arm. Finally, after the hot sweats and pain subsided, I crawled back into bed exhausted and waited for sleep to take me. When the morning broke, I was amazed I slept at all. Even a hot shower didn't wash the sense of foreboding away. I wanted to scream. "Why—me, again!"

CHAPTER SEVEN

On the night of the fire, the police questioned me after the ambulance took Wendy away, but what could I tell them? A few weeks later, I received a phone call requesting my presence at the police station for further questioning. Unfortunately, my mother-in-law, Joyce, took the call.

"Blake, the police. They've been trying to get hold of you," she said with an air of disbelief in her tone.

As I took the phone from her, I felt my in-law's eyes watching me intensely. "Yes, of course, I'll come and see you. Anything to help. May I ask what has happened? Yes, I understand. Okay. Yes, ten o'clock will be fine."

As Joyce took the phone from me, my father-in-law patted my shoulder reassuringly and said, "Don't worry, son, I will be with you."

I nodded. "Not that I need one, but it's quite handy having a solicitor to hand," I said with a nervous laugh.

"Please don't worry, Blake. The police have a way of making you feel guilty, even though you've done nothing wrong," Joyce said.

I wasn't so sure. Maybe, my indiscretion revealed itself. After breakfast, Roger and I travelled to the police station in his car. Even if I wanted to go alone, I wasn't in a fit state. I had popped some extra strong headache pills to alleviate tension at the base of my skull. The pills had caused trembling hands and brain fog in me.

"Thank you for coming in, Mr Cobden," said Detective Sergeant Duncan. "We would like you to take a look at a video."

"My son-in-law hasn't done anything wrong," Roger said, more as a question than a statement.

"No, he hasn't, as far as we know, Mr Harcourt."

"What is it you want me to see?" I asked as my father-in-law tried to outstare DS Duncan.

"The security company working for your employer has forwarded a video to us. It's interesting."

The hair on the back of my neck prickled as my mouth dried. If DS Duncan questioned me, I couldn't answer him. I kept my eyes on his, not to outstare him, but so he could see I had nothing to hide. I feared my face displayed my guilt.

"Are we all ready?" he asked his team.

"Could I have some water, please?" I snapped, hoping to delay the moment they started the video.

"Of course." Duncan nodded to his colleague, who hurried away. "You have nothing to worry about Mr Cobden. As you will see, we have confirmation you were where you said when the fire began." He smiled, but it didn't touch his dark grey eyes.

The officer returned with some bottled water and a paper cup. As I broke the bottle seal, my hand shook. Duncan had turned to signal to his colleague to begin the video. Fearing my anxiety would betray me, I sipped the water.

The video from my employer's lift showed me entering with my phone in hand as I texted Wendy to say I was on my way home. The clock in the video matched the time I sent the message. Over the last few weeks, I've replayed the scene endlessly, wishing I had just gone home.

The lift door opened on the next floor down, and Caroline entered. She nodded in my direction, but I gave her no more than a cursory glance as I concentrated on texting. Caroline betrayed no emotions as she turned her back to me and pressed the panel for the ground floor. We exchanged no words until leaving the lift. Caroline grabbed my hand. A bolt of electricity travelled up my arm as her fingers touched, leaving me stunned.

"Come with me, Blake," she mouthed her lips barely moving.

I sipped the water, expecting to see the scene played out before everyone in the room, but it wasn't there. I wanted a replay, but how could I ask without signing a guilty plea?

In the video, we crossed the car park towards Caroline's vehicle. I'm behind her. From the angle of the camera, we're not together, almost disinterested in each other. The next shot showed her Range Rover leaving the car park, closely followed by another dark car, easily mistaken for mine. No number plate was visible. Unbeknownst to me, a blind spot in the underground car park concealed the fact I had left with her. Nor had it shown my return half an hour later to collect my car. The next video the police showed us was of me at the service station.

The Friday rush hour out of the city absorbed my wasted half hour between leaving the office, the service station and getting home. I looked up and met Duncan's eyes. As though he read my mind, he asked, "Is there anything you want to add?"

"No, don't think so."

"You look as though you've remembered something?"

"Remembered? Not really. The video reminded me just how mundane the day started—"

"What are you getting at?" Roger arched his brow at Duncan while placing his hand reassuringly on my arm. I recognised the growing anger in his eyes.

"We're hoping Mr Cobden can tell us more about Caroline Ravenglass?"

"Caroline?" I shook my head. "My boss can tell you more than I can. We work at the same company. That's about it."

"How well did you know her?"

"Of course, I knew of her in passing. Unless you went around with your eyes closed. As you can see on the video, she's a striking woman, but we didn't chat in person." I wanted to suggest they spoke to all the other men in the office but decided it sounded rather bitchy, and might easily backfire.

"Did you know she's missing?"

"Missing? No. You mean missing when no one knows of her whereabouts? I'm doing my best to stay focused on my work to worry about Ms Ravenglass. My colleagues are avoiding me, maybe, too embarrassed by what has happened to my family. Too afraid I'll burst into tears if they speak to me."

Duncan smirked, but his eyes spoke volumes. I hoped he hadn't read the relief on my face when I saw the camera hadn't picked up my leaving with her. The fifteen wasted minutes, I would never get back, along with my family. The guilt haunted me. If I hadn't stopped for sex or to recharge my car, would I have arrived home soon enough to make a difference?

The police reassured me; the fire was well established and the heat too intense for me to save them.

CHAPTER EIGHT

"Wendy, where are you?" I called while pushing all thoughts of four years ago to the back of my mind. In the fast-fading light, the dilapidated house was full of shadows. On the landing, through a gap in a broken window, black clouds rolled across the far horizon, drawing in the bright blue sky that had welcomed our arrival at the house. I paused at the top of the stairs, listening, unsure whether to hunt for Wendy downstairs or to continue looking for her in the rest of the monstrosity. I knew her curiosity drove her on to explore without me.

Just as I decided to return to the kitchen, a door slammed above me. I hurried along the landing, pushing open doors, hoping to find my way up to the next floor. On turning a corner, I found another flight of stairs. Hesitation made me reach for my phone as I checked to see if the stairs could bear my weight. I switched the phone to torch and took the steps one at a time. At the top of the stairs, a door stood ajar.

"Wendy?" I called, pushing it open.

As my fingertips made contact, my shoulder muscles convulsed. A throbbing pain tore through me. I dropped to my knees. The attic door swung inwards, and through my tears, two shadowy figures moved towards me, arms outstretched, highlighted against the dying sun that burst through an oval window, filling the room with a blinding light.

Once again, the nightmare raced back to me. The dusty space smelt of burning flesh smoke and melting plastic while the sounds of the endless screaming and shattering glass filled my mind. I covered my ears. Something primaeval shook within me. From my gut, a spasm transformed into a sound that filled my whole being before travelling to my mouth and exploding into the room. "Noo!"

"Daddy—Daddy—" With melted faces, they held their red-raw arms towards me. "Daddy, help us—we need you!"

I struggled to breathe as an acrid smell overwhelmed me. I lowered my head and charged at the two figures. They dissolved. A moth-eaten lace curtain crumbled into a swirling dust cloud, illuminated by the window. The dancing particles set off a coughing fit as I fought for air. Fear bubbled inside me as I struggled to draw in the fresh air. A thunderous boom echoed overhead, followed closely by what sounded like gravel thrown at the roof. As my coughing subsided, I realised it was raining. The settling dust revealed a leak in the roof. I watched in fascination as the remnants of the curtains darkened as water trickled across the floor. That's when I saw the footprints.

There were two sets. Neither belonged to my imaginary children or me. I was sure of that much as the water washed them away. Had Wendy met someone up here before I had arrived? Possibly another woman, but why? I hurried down to the ground floor, calling as I went.

CHAPTER NINE

I felt like an impostor, my mind too focused on my betrayal. There was no one to talk to about my feelings, so I bottled it up and spent time at Wendy's bedside to escape the in-laws. They told me Wendy wouldn't want to replace our daughters. I bit my tongue. It wasn't any of their business. The thought hadn't even crossed my mind, especially while dealing with my grief alone. The company I worked for allowed me compassionate leave, but my in-laws' sorrow saturated me to the point where I couldn't breathe.

Wendy's large private room became my sanctuary. More like a hotel suite than a hospital bedroom, it gave me a space to breathe and think. If there had been a spare bed, I would have slept there too. On entering the suite, a shower room and toilet were on the left. Opposite was a door into a small kitchenette with a tiny fridge where visitors could make drinks. The soft grey lush carpet contrasted beautifully with the lime green walls while the delicate flora curtains, matching cushion covers and bed cover picked out the grey and lime green. A light-grey leather sofa faced a television screen on the wall opposite the bed. The only difference from a hotel was the cameras watching us and the steady beeping of the machines wired up to Wendy.

Sun flooded the room as I entered, carrying fresh flowers to replace the ones beside her bed. At first, the hospital sedated Wendy. I had protested, wanting her to know the girls were gone. My in-laws busied themselves planning the children's funerals as though they knew what we wanted for them. Wendy's parents felt she needed more time to recover so she never attended her daughters' funerals. I felt this would set her back months, if not a lifetime. The grandparents agreed to allow Tina and Alex to be together in their final resting place so that when Wendy had recovered, she could lay flowers across their grave.

After disposing of the old flowers in the kitchenette, I placed the fresh ones on a chest of drawers where Wendy could see them. Since losing our daughters, fine lines had appeared around her eyes and mouth while silver threads showed in her hairline around her temples. Upon entering the room, Wendy never responded to me. Maybe she did when I wasn't around. Her parents and the nursing staff only said, "There was no change," or "As well as can be expected."

My wife stared blankly at the ceiling, looking ghostly pale beneath the sheets. I kissed her cold cheek before settling in the comfy chair beside the bed. I kept the chat bright and breezy. I always started with the weather, followed by how her parents and I were coping. Then I would read from the local newspaper, telling her my opinions, hoping to get a reaction from her. The only time a glimmer of change registered on her face was while I shared updates from the police about the fire. The lines became deeper on her face as if she was in pain. The heart monitor's lines never changed and continued to race on. Finally, when I ran out of things to say, I would stare out the window and go back over everything that had happened.

*

The bleeping sound of the monitor and Wendy's steady breathing became the background sound to my thoughts as I picked over the recent events. I wanted to beg for Wendy's forgiveness, to take her in my arms, and kiss her tears away. She was my world, all I ever wanted. Caroline was nothing. Tears rolled down my cheeks, I brushed them away. The steadily flashing red light on the camera made me wonder whether someone was watching me. Did they think I was crying in frustration for my sick wife or maybe for myself? I turned to the window again and studied the view of the parkland and beyond.

How could I put the truth into words so Wendy could understand when she woke into our nightmare? Would she forgive me if I did?

"Maybe—" I said aloud as the sky darkened. A cloud crossed the sun causing it to disappear from view, leaving only racing shadows across the trees and flowerbeds outside. In the brief darkness, the light of reality shone. If I told Wendy the truth, what would there be to gain? The fifteen minutes could easily be explained away by simply saying I was stuck in traffic, so with nothing to gain, why add to her hurt?

Anyway, what about the unanswered questions buzzing around my head? Where was Wendy when the fire started? Why didn't she save the girls while saving herself? Something didn't add up.

CHAPTER TEN

As the sun burst from behind the clouds, it reminded me of our wedding day. Wendy had carefully planned the whole event. We needed to stand before the church altar and speak our vows to each other as the sun flooded through the stained-glass window. Only the sun at the crucial moment let her down. Wendy gripped my hand tightly as she uttered the words, staring not into my eyes but at the stained-glass window.

On leaving the church porch, the overcast sky brightened. Tears ran down Wendy's cheek and melted my heart as we stepped into a beam of golden sunlight as the clouds parted. I brushed her tears away with my thumbs while leaning in to kiss her. "Hey, my beautiful lady, don't cry. Not on our wedding day."

Thirteen years ago seemed a lifetime away as I stared at the racing cloud as Wendy slept on in her sedation. I recalled the moment I brushed the tears from her cheeks. There had been something about her face. A flash of recognition. At the time, I thought the sunlight was playing tricks on me. A shadow distorted Wendy's face into another's. I held their face in my hands with the tenderness I had felt for my new wife. Only what I had seen in the other woman's dark eyes was such coldness I hastily stepped back from her.

"Blake, are you alright?" Wendy's face reappeared before me.

I took hold of her hand and as I turned from her, I said to her family and friends. "Now, I think we all could do with a drink, don't you?"

As their cheers filled the air, everyone dashed to their waiting cars and headed to our reception at a local hotel.

*

One morning, not so long after we were married, my wife took delivery of a parcel just as I was coming down the stairs.

"Oh, Blake, it's our wedding photographs." Wendy hurried to the lounge, dropped onto the sofa, and placed the parcel on the coffee table. She patted the cushion next to her and said, "Come and sit with me before you rush off to work. I want us to look at them together."

I checked my watch, wanting to wait until we had more time in the evening, but my wife's excitement was uncontainable.

"Grab a knife, Blake," she said while tearing at the box.

"Be careful." I handed it to her.

Wendy slipped the blade under one end of the box and pulled it towards her. I held my breath.

"Stop it! You're making me nervous," She turned the box around and did the same again. Then she stabbed the knife into the top of the box, yanking it towards her. The blade bounced off the tape and caught her other hand. She seemed frozen, not screaming or reacting until blood oozed from some nicks in the top of two fingers. "Fucking hell, look what you made me do!" She sat down with a thud, pushing her fingers into her mouth.

I rushed into the kitchen, grabbed a roll of paper and some plasters, and went to help Wendy.

"Get off," she yelled, looking at her fingers. "I can sort myself out."

I left her to it and finished opening the box. I scooped the photo album, wrapped in tissue paper, laid it before her, and then took the box and the knife into the kitchen.

"Dear God!" Wendy's annoyance followed me.

On re-entering the lounge, I found Wendy flicking the pages of the album, her jaw set, lips pencil thin. "All our photos are ruined." She looked up, her eyes filled with tears.

"Why didn't you just wait...?" I said, expecting to see blood. It wasn't Wendy's bloody fingerprints that had ruined our photographs. Instead of photos of my wife, someone had superimposed a ghostly image of another woman. I picked up the album and studied it closely. "It isn't possible."

"What isn't?" Wendy got up from the sofa and snatched up the phone.

"What made the photographer think we would accept this, after all the money we paid? It's fucking rubbish!"

"Please don't keep swearing. It isn't like you. There won't be anyone there now. You'll have to wait until it opens at nine."

"It's bloody disgusting."

I snapped some pictures with my phone and then zoomed in on one of the images. The same face, I had seen on our wedding day stared back at me. Who was she? Why us?

"I'll call in at the studio on my way to work; they'll have some explaining to do," Wendy picked up the album and carried it to the kitchen. The tissue paper lay crumpled on the floor, forgotten.

*

At lunchtime, I received a call from Wendy. Phoning each other at work was something we rarely did.

"Blake, can you message me over the photos you took of the album this morning, please."

"What's happened?"

"I'm in the studio with the photographer. He's looking at the album. All the photographs look stunningly beautiful. I want to show him what we saw."

"Hang on, a second." I switched my phone on and paged through the photos I had snapped. All I saw was Wendy's smiling face. "Wendy, there's noth—"

"Please, don't say it, Blake. I'm feeling stupid enough as it is."

"Wendy—"

She was gone.

I was about to close my phone when I rechecked the photos and nearly dropped my phone. The blurred images were back. I paged through them. "Who the hell are you?" I said, staring at a wicked smile playing across pencil-thin lips and in the eyes, a knowing glint shone.

My beautiful wife no longer leaned against me in her wedding dress, all smiles just for me, but the ghostly image of another woman. A woman I didn't know then but I do now.

CHAPTER ELEVEN

Five months after the fire, I decided I needed to make a farewell visit to the house I once called home for thirteen precious years. Wendy was about to leave the hospital, so I decided before she came home; I would visit. It saved me from lying to her about where I was going or had been.

I arrived late in the afternoon to avoid meeting any of my old neighbours, knowing they would still be at work, as I wanted to spend the time there alone with my thoughts. To avoid anyone seeing me, I parked several roads away from the cul-de-sac and took the footpath that ran around the back of the properties. The path brought me to a wooded area at the back of my old home. I stared at the burnt-out shell that was once our forever home. The roof was gone, and only three outer walls remained standing. It was hard to believe it had once been a home filled with the sounds of childish laughter and Christmas trees in the hall. All those happy memories were just dust now.

Once only green lawns surrounded the house, but now a high metal fence enclosed it, put up by the insurance company, no doubt. At the front of the house, the carefully nurtured shrubs, lawns, and flower borders no longer had me to tend to them. Even after the intense heat, nature quickly reclaimed the site. The over-grown hedges shielded the sadness of my ruined home from the other houses around it. Outside of the fence, under the watchful eye of my neighbour Jack, he tended to the lawns between the neighbours' homes and mine.

At least my girls had a memorable beginning in life, brought up in a loving home and cared for by parents who loved each other. My unusual start in life never bothered me. My life began when I met Wendy, though this was never enough for her. Her intentions came from a good place. She believed if I knew who my parents were; their reason for not claiming me would give me closure.

*

"I've been thinking," she said on my arrival home from work one day. "We should track down your foster brother and invite him and if he has a family to stay with us. He might remember something important that can help us find your parents."

"I know all there is to know about my family, Wendy," I said as I went into the kitchen to see if she had started dinner.

"I'm not talking about your foster parents," she called after me.

"As far as I'm concerned Reg and Dora were my parents. Why should I care about them, Wendy, when they never cared about me? To leave a child alone beside a river was crazy. I'm thankful every day to the fisherman who found me."

"But, Blake, you don't know their side of the story." She rose unsteadily from the sofa, her belly hard and round, and reached for me.

"No, I haven't started dinner yet. I couldn't motivate myself."

"It's all right." I kissed the top of her head.

"Blake, there might be a good reason for your parents not being with you."

"Wendy, I've dealt with this—"

"Please think about it. You have no memory of where you came from or even who you were before you were found—maybe it's the same for them. I've been thinking—"

"You should be thinking about our child," I rested my hand on her stomach. Our child floating in water reminded me of my rebirth. Maybe that's what it was. I was reborn. I lifted her head and stared into her hopeful eyes. "You and this baby are my family."

Wendy's eyes darkened, and I looked away. The look that clouded her eyes, if I lingered too long would transform into another. "Let me get changed, and I'll order a takeaway."

"I'm sorry dinner isn't ready, but I felt sick."

"It's no problem. You're both okay?"

"Yes, we're fine. What about DNA testing?"

"God—no! Who knows what that might throw up?"

"Aren't you curious about where you came from and your parentage?"

"After thirty years of not knowing, I'm happy with the here and now."

"But it's important, if—anything—you know." Wendy rubbed her stomach.

"Let's deal with that when the situation arises, shall we."

*

Wendy kept chipping away at my guilt with her obsession with my past until it began to drive a wedge between us. Soon after the birth of our first child, who thankfully arrived perfect in every way, Wendy dropped the subject of DNA testing, as her priorities shifted to the baby and house hunting for our first home together.

I left my wife to find our perfect home though her choice left me feeling a little on edge for some reason. She had a thing for the old properties, saying they had more style and character.

"They have more of a beating heart," she said. "An untold story of lives they've sheltered under their roofs."

"They are vacant for a good reason, like dodgy wiring, woodworm, leaking roof, so they're endless money pits and not environmentally friendly either."

"So, nothing that can't be sorted."

"I might be earning good money, but our daughter's needs must come first. It will be cold and damp until we can pay for the repairs and fit modern central heating."

"Okay, I understand." Wendy hugged Alex to her and kissed her tiny fingers. "Daddy is right. Mummy needs to think about you. Anyway, I haven't found the right house yet, Blake, but you might like this one."

I took the property details Wendy handed me. The house was a large, modern, three-bedroom property in a cul-de-sac. The picture looked inviting, but estate agents always made houses look fabulous.

"Google it," Wendy called to me from the bathroom. "They do a tour of it. You'll see it's just right for us."

*

Wendy was right. On entering the house, it became home. Maggie and Jack, our new neighbours, welcomed us in with a cake, and fresh milk, in case we forgot to bring some. While Wendy and I unpacked boxes, our neighbours put a kettle on and carried the boxes marked for the kitchen through to start sorting things out in there. Wendy and Maggie clicked straightaway. Maggie wasn't pushy and always asked whether there was anything she could do to help. In a way, I adopted Maggie, or possibly, she adopted us, becoming a stand-in for my parents or at least a surrogate grandmother for me.

Maggie was easy to talk to and soon learnt about my past or lack of it. She persuaded me I should investigate the mystery of my early life. Wendy was delighted. I felt less pressured this time. Perhaps the birth of my children changed my point of view, making it more about their benefit than mine. In the future, they would ask questions about their other grandparents; at least I could tell them, with some certainty, exactly why I didn't know.

"Blake, I have a friend who could help you," Maggie said. "I know you weren't adopted, but he specialises in tracking adopted children's birthmothers. I could ask him over to give you some advice."

"It can't do any harm," Wendy said.
*

I agreed. I had nothing to lose. If Dora couldn't uncover anything more at the time, then Maggie's friend still wouldn't be able to solve the mystery thirty years later.

We all sat in the lounge watching Robert Bridges, a thin stick of a man. He sat stiffly in an armchair; his gold-framed glasses perched on the end of his narrow nose as he delicately picked up the cuttings. After placing them in date order, he pulled out his phone and photographed them. Wendy returned from the kitchen with a tray of drinks. "Would you like tea or coffee, Robert?"

Robert dismissed her with a slight hand gesture and without looking up from his task. Maggie, Wendy, and I sat hugging our drinks in silence. Suddenly, Robert cleared his throat with a light cough.

"Well," Robert said, plucking his glasses from the end of his nose. "Not a lot to go on here?"

"It's all I have."

"Hmm, it would be wise to do a DNA test to see if we can discover any new links. Things have come a long way in thirty years."

"My parents are possibly dead by now."

"That may be so, but it could uncover other family members." Robert pulled a test kit from his briefcase and set it on the table.

Wendy gave a light giggle. I smiled at her excitement. When she smiled back at me, it wasn't her, but the ghostly image of the woman with steely, cold eyes.

Was she haunting me?

A wave of vulnerability swept over me. I turned back to Robert. "So, what do I have to do?"

Once Robert had my spit, he said, "You might not hear from me for a while as we have little information. I'll recheck the sites your foster mother had access to, with any that weren't available to her.

At the front door, we said our goodbyes. Robert turned to Wendy and me as Maggie walked back to her house. "Once we get your DNA test result, then I shall let you know if I've anything new to report. You must realise there's a backlog with DNA testing, so don't expect to hear straightaway. It's such a fascinating case, Mr and Mrs Cobden. Goodbye until we speak again."

*

Three months later, Robert phoned. Maggie had just arrived with one of her lovely cakes and so heard the results with us. Wendy and Maggie sat on the sofa as I placed the phone, on speaker, on the coffee table before us. I sat ready to hear the awful truth, knowing deep inside I was happy to be the person Reg and Dora brought me up to be.

"To start with, Mr Cobden, I haven't uncovered any new information. The police report is the same as the newspapers' reporting on the case. The area they found you in has a long history. In the late 1700s, a dispute broke out between two wealthy branches of the same family that owned Thimble Island, or maybe, the house. It's unclear what the discourse was about, but the land remains unclaimed, and no one has the right to buy it."

"But what has this to do with me?" I asked.

"Nothing really. It's just intriguing. Anyway, I came across another curious, but unrelated fact. Another mystery connected to that particular area. During the falling out over Thimble Island a man went missing about the same time as you."

"Same time as Blake—do you mean on the same day or month he was found, Robert?" Maggie shook her head at me.

I shrugged.

"Yes, the same day, and month, not 1993 I checked old newspaper articles in case your foster mother missed something."

"And you searched until 1820?"

"No. On the same page, reporting your rescue was a column called *On This Day*—which listed past events the newspapers have reported on over the last two hundred and fifty years."

"Interesting, I suppose. Do you have any other news for me?

"Your DNA results haven't given us any living relatives, I'm afraid."

"Oh, so am I British?" I laughed.

"Yes, with a hint of Anglo-Saxon and Celtic. I'm sorry, I've been of no further help to you."

"It's okay. Thank you for trying."

"Goodbye."

"So, you're still my man of mystery," Wendy said. "And I love you all the more for it."

CHAPTER TWELVE

I wanted to weep as I took in our fire-damaged home, not for the loss of material things but for my girls and our contented life. The roof was gone, and all that remained was an empty shell. With a struggle, I climbed through a child-size hole in the fence and crunched over the broken glass before entering what had once been the kitchen. The acrid smell of smoke still lingered there. A few melted cupboards hung on the walls, stained black by the smoke. I recalled Wendy poring over catalogue after catalogue online, notepad in hand, trying to make her choice for the new kitchen. It took her weeks to settle on the one she wanted.

The fire had taken less time to destroy it. The report into the fire stated it began on the ground floor, in the corner of the hall. The stairs had acted like a chimney drawing it up to the next floor.

At the top of the stairs, the smoke entered my eldest daughter's bedroom, causing her to pass away in her sleep. I hoped it was true. Next was the family bathroom before Tina's room. Next to Alex's bedroom was my office before the large master bedroom that sat above the garage. In the report, the fire source was near the front door. It puzzled me; apart from twinkling lights around the porch, nothing in the hall was flammable. It seemed more logical if the fire started in the garage because of the number of chemicals, half-empty paint tins, oils, and car cleaning products I kept there.

I moved into the hallway. The glass-fronted porch was gone. What remained suffered damage by the smoke and water. Charred remains of familiar things littered the ground beneath my feet. Heaped in one corner, scorched picture frames that once held the snapshots of our lives, the glass, and photos were long gone. On the day of the fire, all I was wearing were the clothes I had. My stained shirt stunk of Caroline, our rough sex and her cheap perfume. No one else noticed the mud, cooking oil, and fast-food grease staining my trousers and jacket in the chaos.

I just thanked whatever deity was watching over me that I had taken my work's laptop and had my phone on me that awful day, as I had kept my family photos and videos in a special folder. When the time was right and I could bring myself to look on their smiling faces once again, I would, but for now, it was too painful.

"Whoever you are, you shouldn't be in there," a voice snarled at me.

I stepped out of the house and came face to face with my old neighbour.

"Oh, Mr Cobden. Please accept my apology," he said, his cheeks colouring.

"No, don't, Jack. Glad someone is keeping an eye on the place. I just came for some closure."

Jack nodded his understanding, though he studied me intently. He gave a nervous cough, something he always did. If you knew him well enough, you knew it was a sign that he had more to say.

I waited.

"Didn't the fire investigators discover what happened then?"

"Yes, but none of it makes any sense to me. You know how it is. You feel as though being at the place where it happened will somehow give you the answers you're searching for, or at least clear up some nagging questions."

"I know what you mean. Come. Have a drink with me, lad." Jack turned away. I struggled through the gap again and followed him across the expanse of lawn that separated our two houses and entered his by the back door.

The layout of our two homes was identical. Sitting in the open-planned kitchen, with a clear view of the hall, I tried to visualize how the fire could have started and spread so quickly. I knew Wendy would've been ready to go by the time she had text to ensure I was leaving on time. After Caroline had dumped me in the alleyway, I switched my phone back on and discovered a missed call from her, along with some texts.

"How's your lovely wife coping, lad?" Jack interrupted my thoughts as he handed me a mug of coffee.

"Still at the clinic but should be out soon if all goes well."

"These things all take time. Maggie and I still can't rid our minds of the awful wailing sound your wife made as she screamed for help," Jack said, pushing the biscuit tin towards me. "Help yourself, lad."

"Yes, it must have been very frightening for you both seeing her trapped and unable to help." I took a sip of the coffee. Its bitter taste caught me unaware as much as Jack's puzzled look.

"Trapped? No, Wendy wasn't trapped. Your daughters were."

I lowered my cup. "She was outside when the fire started?" I tried to keep my voice level.

"Maggie saw her from our bedroom window. She stood beside her car as though waiting for someone. The door was open, engine running. Odd, we thought. Who leaves their car running? Not good for the environment." Jack gave me a sideward glance.

"Wendy was due to go out. I was stuck in traffic."

"Oh, I see. Still seems odd. She should've waited in the house with the girls. Anyway, who takes an overnight case with them for an evening out?"

"Overnight case."

"Yes, Maggie said Wendy looked to be leaving—" Jack coughed and then corrected himself. "Or maybe going away for the weekend. We weren't spying on your wife, Blake. Maggie was in the bedroom when she saw the event unfold."

"Jack, I'm sure you and Maggie were just concerned neighbours. Who unfortunately witnessed a terrible event."

"That happened not long after the other vehicle arrived. We saw it wasn't yours. You park in front of the garage. This one swung around in front of Wendy's car, blocking her. A tall woman climbed out and tried to embrace Wendy, but she pushed her away. Wendy gesticulated a lot and seemed angry. The woman tried to hold your wife, but she wasn't having any of it. Wendy kept pointing to the woman's vehicle as though telling her to go. She pointed at her wrist and then at the house. After an exchange of words, your wife stormed into the house, and the woman followed her. More shouting ensued, but the words weren't clear enough for us to hear. The next moment Wendy came charging out. She leaned into the car, killed the engine, pulled out the case, and set it down on the road before dragging out her handbag. She had her back to the house, talking on her phone. Maggie saw something was wrong before Wendy did. She called me upstairs to clarify her worst fears—" Jack's voice faulted.

"What was it?" My stomach clenched as my hand shook, spilling drops of dark coffee on the pine table. I set the cup down and wiped it with my elbow, not that Jack had noticed.

"A bright glow." Jack's eyes focused on the past, reliving the event second by second.

Questions filled my mind and lingered on my tongue, but I said nothing, willing him to continue. Finally, he exhaled. His words tumbled over themselves as though he was exorcising his disturbed mind, or maybe, he wanted me to hear his confession.

"The glow was a soft flickering ember in the doorway, like Christmas lights, artificial.

Maggie wanted me to go over, but I didn't think it was right." Jack's eyes clouded as his face took on a pained expression. "Then we saw the smoke billowing out the door. I dashed for my phone and called the fire service. On returning to the window, I saw Wendy trying to get indoors, but the fire held her back. That's when the screaming started."

"You said the other woman was in the house?"

He nodded. "That's the odd thing. We were certain she was inside, but during the chaos, the vehicle disappeared."

"Can you describe her?"

He closed his eyes. "Her height stood out most. Next to Wendy, she was taller, well-dressed, not casual, but smart business-like." He opened his eyes and looked straight at me. "Do you know her?"

I shook my head. "Wendy has friends I don't know. Online friends, for instance, you know, other new mums. You said the vehicle had gone. Did you happen to notice its make?"

"No. I only saw it briefly. It looked large and dark in colour, but our focus was on the house."

"Did you tell the police?"

A look of concern settled on his face. Without breaking eye contact, he rose. "I'm sorry. Please forgive us, but we mind our own business, Mr Cobden. I shouldn't have told you. I was speaking out of turn. Once your lovely wife recovers, she'll explain everything to you."

I pushed my cup towards him and stood. "You're a witness to what happened—"

Jack cut me off by raising his hand. "Like your wife, my wife isn't very well. So, we must ask for your forgiveness," he said, moving towards the front door. I followed him. Jack continued, "We've suffered too, witnessing such a terrible scene. The sounds of Wendy's screaming will never leave us."

"Jack—I'm—"

"Thank you," he said. Not understanding that I wasn't forgiving him but questioning why I should.

"One other thing I must ask of you if you come back here to live," Jack's smile broadened, but it didn't touch his eyes. "Please don't ever mention our conversation to my wife. What happened over there," he nodded towards my old home. "Was very disturbing for us all, Mr Cobden. I advised my wife that speaking out would do more harm than good. You understand, don't you? Goodbye," he said and closed the door.

Uncertain of what Jack implied, I stared blankly at the front door. A slight movement in the curtain above told me Maggie had heard everything. I nodded in her direction. She gave a half smile and let the curtain drop. She, more than anyone, was entitled to my forgiveness. She loved my girls as if they were her own, the children she never had. In my heart, I knew she would blame herself for not doing more. As I drove off, a bitter taste filled my mouth and it wasn't Jack's disgusting cheap coffee but my anger bubbling up. After Jack's comments, I knew we wouldn't return.

*

Within the first six months after leaving the hospital, Wendy began to recover something of her old self, but I knew we had a long way to go. A year later, my wife seemed ready to find a new place. I arrived home from work and found her sitting on the bed in our squashed little room.

"I hated this room even as a child and hate it even more now," she said, without welcoming me home or looking up from her laptop. "I printed these up today. Could we take a look at them soon?"

I pulled my jacket off, sat down, and went to kiss her forehead, but she turned away. One step at a time, I told myself. "Let's see what you have here." I leaned back against the headboard. Wendy had lost weight, her curves with it. Her cheeks were hollow, her mouth a thin-pinched line. My only wish now was to have my beautiful wife back again, to see her smile, and hear her laughter. We looked at quite a few detached houses that were on the market, but nothing got Wendy excited until one day.

"I've found it, Blake, our forever home. You'll love it as much as me, I'm sure. It's called Estuary Hall.

CHAPTER THIRTEEN

Outside, the first rumbles of thunder echoed, seeming to shake the very foundations of the dilapidated house. I needed to find my wife and get the hell out of it. I hurried along the landing, calling her name while opening the bedroom doors. I pushed all thoughts of the past behind me as I shouted into the dark, dank rooms filled with the depressing odour of decay and shifting shadows. The neglected bedrooms echoed their unhappiness, highlighted by the torch beam. The dusty floors showed no signs that Wendy had entered any rooms beyond the master bedroom. I made my way back along the corridor just as the house seemed to come alive with the sound of the wind entering uninvited through the broken windows and missing roof tiles.

"Wendy, where are you?"

Through the cacophony of creaks and moans, I couldn't hear Wendy answering me. The wind and rain rattled the windows and raced around the chimneys as I dashed to the top of the main stairs calling as I went.

The darkness seemed to suck me in as I clung to the handrail, fearing the steps might not take my weight. The banister felt familiar as I slid my hand slowly along its smooth surface. My fingertips seemed to recognise each knot in the wood. The feeling caught me unaware, making my heart shudder. Why was it so recognisable? Wendy eager to see upstairs hadn't allowed us time to study the staircase or to comment on the ornate banister, on our way up. "Where are you, Wendy?"

The howling wind drowned out my calls. On entering the kitchen, a flash of lightning briefly lit up the dark room allowing me to see a figure seated at a table.

"Didn't you hear me calling?" I said. My anger, not helped by the throbbing of my damaged hand, revealed itself in the tone of my voice. I tried to peer through the gaps in the boarded window. Outside, the raging storm had taken all visibility away. Wendy let out a deep sigh, causing me to turn to her. What I was about to say would destroy the bridges I'd built to save our marriage. "I'm sorry Wendy, but this house will suck us dry. We should never have come here. Let's get out of here. Tomorrow, we'll look at the other houses you've selected."

"Well, unfortunately, you have no choice in the matter. After all the fun, I've had to get you back here, you're not going anywhere." The voice that filled the darkness ripped my heart apart.

"What—What are you doing here?"

"Let's say we've some unfinished business, Blake." The ghostly figure of Caroline rose from behind the table and moved towards me. Something in the way she moved sent a wave of nausea through me. Another flash of lightning lit up the kitchen, creating shadows across Caroline's countenance. I realised now why she had always seemed somehow familiar to me, the unconscious reason I had avoided her at work until that fateful day she entered the lift. Caroline Ravenglass haunted me. The shadowy figure in the wedding photograph stood before me. In some unfathomable way, the house and Caroline were one. "I've nothing to say to you," I said with malice.

"Who said anything about talking, Blake? It's too late for that."

I stepped back. "How did you find us here?"

"Us here? There's no us here. Just you and me."

"No, my wife's here—"

"Your wife." She gave a peal of hollow laughter. It echoed around us. "If you're talking about that pathetic woman called Wendy. Then I hate to tell you, she left you ages ago."

"No. She's here."

"You're not so sure now, are you? You were always full of bullshit, Blake. Soon you will remember me and this house?" She spread her arms.

"Me—Remember this house? I've never been here before. My wife found it online one evening."

"Can you be so sure, Blake?" Caroline lifted her arms. With a wave of her hands, the room became flooded with light. The windows shone with sunlight that I had to shield my eyes. The pain in my shoulder intensified. The sparsely furnished kitchen was free of dust, cobwebs, and dirt, while the flagstone floor looked new. Caroline gave a half smile.

"Soon you will remember me and all that went before." In the harsh light, her eyes narrowed, and her lips became thin black lines of pure hatred. "I gave you everything when we built our home here together." She gestured to the room.

"That's impossible. It's over two hundred years old." I backed away from her, caught my heel on something, and fell backwards. I tried to regain my balance by twisting sideways. As my palms made contact with the wall, they vanished through it. Too slow to react, I sunk into what I can only describe as jelly. The pulsing mass constricted, making it hard for me to breathe. A pain shot through my birthmark like a bolt of electricity.

"Stop struggling and relax," Caroline's voice came from afar. "The house will help you to remember just who you are."

CHAPTER FOURTEEN

The tightness in my chest lessened, and I gasped, drawing in air as quickly as I could. Once my breathing eased, I became aware of a sweet earthy perfume, like freshly cut grass, and a low buzzing sound that seemed to encircle me. My mind screamed sensory overload and to flee.

On opening my eyes, I was lying on my back among tall grasses and meadow flowers. They towered over me, a swaying kaleidoscope of colours. A sweet symphony of buzzing insects and gently lapping water calmed my racing heart. The blue sky seemed to go on forever. I watched, in fascination, as fluffy white clouds came into view. Finally, I felt relaxed enough to risk sitting up. Pain shot up my arm as I put weight on my right hand. I hugged my shoulder and looked down. Under my shirt, a cream-coloured bandage wrapped around my torso, held a padding of gauze in place. The throbbing in my arm travelled down to my fingers. The middle fingernail was black and oozed pus, but the question I needed answered the most was—where the fuck was I?

The warmth from the ground penetrated my body, adding to my confusion. The amount of rain that had fallen should have saturated the ground. The sun felt too warm on my back as I rose and took in the surroundings. The landscape was stunningly beautiful as tall trees embraced the skyline while reeds and grasses hugged the water's edge. The humming insects encircled me as I knelt to scoop up the crystal-clear water to rinse my face and hands. The temptation to drink it was overpowering, but I let the water trickle through my fingers as the sound of beating wings and splashing made me look up. A flock of waterfowl took noisily to the sky, filling it with movement. It seemed so surreal. I reached for my phone, only to find it was gone, along with my pocket too. I no longer wore jeans or trainers but breeches and knee-high boots. I hadn't noticed earlier that my jacket and t-shirt were gone and had been replaced with just a white cotton shirt with long sleeves rolled back. How was that possible?

Before me was a well-trodden path. I followed it, hoping to find someone to show me back to my car. I walked on for a few minutes, hearing nothing but insects, bird songs, and wildfowl above the tall reeds and grasses. The path opened onto a stretch of freshly mowed lawn that sloped down to the water's edge. Above me, on a stone patio, a house stood towering over the landscape. I recognised it, though it wasn't in the condition Wendy and I had seen it. The sunlight glinted off the polished glass in the windows, the freshly painted eves, and the newly tiled roof and gothic towers and the new stonework it wasn't so much as newly-repaired but a brand-new house.

Stunned by the house, I tried to take in its beauty, and then became aware of someone calling my name. I shielded my eyes and turned towards the estuary. The sunlight glistening on the water made it hard to see who was calling. Then a shape appeared out of the shadows on the path and came towards me. A woman held a straw bonnet to her head with one hand, its ribbons floating over her shoulders. On such a hot day, it seemed odd that she wore a seventeenth-century style, ankle-length gown. As the woman slowly made her way along the path, she occasionally lifted her head and gave me a little wave. Something about the way she carried herself reminded me of Caroline. She placed one foot in front of the other in slow, precise steps, like a cat hunting its prey. In such peaceful surroundings, I felt no urge to rush down to meet her or to call out to ask her name. I waited on the stone patio, rolling and stretching my aching shoulder, trying to process the feeling that I had become a chess piece in a game where someone played by their own rules.

The woman called again, her voice soft and intimate, carried to me on the breeze. She took the stone steps slowly, lifting her gown a fraction to reveal slim ankles, enjoying the fact I waited for her. When she came closer, she lifted her face, and our eyes met. My heart pounded. The dream became a nightmare. Caroline's familiar smile stared at me, softened by glossy, bouncing auburn ringlets. She could have easily been an actor in a period drama. Gone were the layers of makeup, lipstick, and nail varnish. The freshness in her face gave her a look of innocence.

"Oh, Blake, it is wonderful having you at home at last. For too long I have waited for my dream to come true."

"Dream—Caroline, is this real?" I had to be dreaming, but the breeze that ruffled my hair and cooled my forehead felt real enough to me, along with the sun on my back, the sounds of the birds and insects, and the smell of the estuary.

"No, Blake. You're not dreaming." Caroline gave a light giggle and slipped her arm through mine. "See, do I not feel real to you?"

She did, but she wasn't like the Caroline from my office. Dreams made no sense, did they? The weirdest of things happened in dreams. They had no order to them. "Where are we?" I asked, but somehow, I already knew the answer. In the house, earlier on, as the storm raged outside, Caroline told me the house would explain everything. Of course, that was when I tripped and hit the wall. But, how did that justify the newly repaired building or the reason for Caroline's arrival in fancy dress, behaving as though nothing untoward had passed between us four years ago?

"We are where we have always wanted to be, in our magic kingdom awaiting my father's consent, so we can marry and live happily ever after." Caroline gestured towards the house. "Please, do not upset yourself. Father is impatient to speak with you, today. That's why I came to fetch you. Hopefully, Papa and you will agree on a date this time." She gave a childish giggle.

"A wedding—" I shook my head. "None of this is real. I'm dreaming. I banged my head when I fell against the wall."

"Do not tease me." She lifted her laughing eyes to mine. "Come; let me show you our beautiful house, Papa built for us."

"Your father had this house built for—us?" A chuckle caught in my throat. It was too crazy for words.

"Yes, is it not wonderful? Almost the castle we dreamed of as children; do you not think so?"

Though the soft curls around her face created a look of innocence, something in her voice, an undertone, reminded me of the office Caroline, the manipulative one that wouldn't take no for an answer. Had I unwittingly become a player in a game of her making? But why? And where was Wendy?

Caroline tugged at my hand. "Let me show you the house. Then you will see how wonderful everything will be once we are married." I followed her along a flagstone path into a freshly laid-out garden. A maze of footpaths led down to a landing stage by the water's edge. Rows of young trees and shrubs followed a fence on the outer edge of the formal garden while bright red terracotta tiles edged flower borders. My mind tried to find some reasonable explanation for it all. Caroline chatted about the wedding plans and which guests we had to invite. I nodded as though I was listening, but my focus was on the house.

We climbed the stone steps that led to the front door. "Caroline, why are you here?" I asked.

"You know why. Papa promised to build us a beautiful house for when you came home." She squeezed my arm, causing me to flinch.

"Oh, I'm such a fool. That's your injured arm." Her smile was too bright, too eager. "You were lucky, not to lose your whole arm. Papa said the infection nearly killed you after the doctor extracted a piece of wood from your shoulder. The cannon fire that destroyed the battlements also killed quite a few members of your regiment. Though you were badly injured, you managed to pull some of your men free. In Papa's eyes, you are quite the hero."

"Cannon fire—battlements—what are you talking about?"

"Please, Blake." Caroline placed her hand gently on my face. Her fingertips were cool to the touch. In a childlike voice, she said, "Please, do not raise your voice to me, especially not in front of our families." She let her hand drop and turned her back to me. Staring across the garden, she continued, "You know how hard it has been for our families since the unfortunate death of my brother." Caroline's voice caught in her throat. She raised a hand to her mouth, and let out a strange sob. It sounded like a strangled laugh.

Compassion overwhelmed me, wanting me to take her in my arms, to comfort her. An image of Wendy with her blackened face, beating my chest as I tried to comfort her, filled my mind. I tried to make sense of the two images. Both seemed surreal. Nothing made any sense. I dropped onto the low brick wall that edged the raised patio area before the large porch. It seemed like an eternity since I took the brick from the crumbling wall to break into the boarded-up building. I wanted to identify the brick as validation that Wendy and I had broken into the building. Of course, it was impossible to know which brick.

The view from the patio was stunning. The blue sky reflected off the clear water of the estuary, while the bright sunshine made it sparkle. I could understand the drive to build such a house here. It dominated the landscape. There wasn't another house for miles. Yet, when Wendy and I had stood in the neglected building, looking across the water, on the far side was a marina full of pleasure yachts and small boats. Where had they gone? I wondered.

"It is only because of the death of my brother, Archie, that Papa has accepted you as the heir to the family fortune. As a woman, he has no desire to see me inherit the family estate. He has no surviving children other than me, unless I married the estate returns to your family along with my father's money. If we marry then he will keep control of everything, including us, too. At least, we can be together."

"Your father isn't happy about us marrying, so why is he accepting it?"

She spun around, raised her chin, and spat the last four words out with such spite I recognised the woman I knew as Caroline. "My happiness is now of importance to him—with my brother dead."

Even though I didn't want to know, I had to ask. "How did your brother die?" A lump of ice expanded in my gut on seeing the fire raging in her eyes, and a smile of delight shaping her lips.

"No need for you to worry about such things, Blake." She patted my arm. "It has been worth it to bring our two families together again and stop all this hatred and fighting over a strip of land once owned by two brothers, a hundred years ago. A foolish bet between themselves has kept our two families apart, and stopped us from marrying."

"Over what?"

"It all started when the two brothers' wives were pregnant, so they made a bet whichever wife gave birth first to a living son would win the land. The land would only revert to the other brother when the last boy of the winning Ravenglass's family died, but only if there was a male heir in the other family of Ravenglass. The land must continue to belong to the family of Ravenglass.

"You're telling me we're related to these brothers?" I glanced up at the house. It must be worth a small fortune—of course, the genealogist, Robert Bridges, had spoken about a feud between influential families over land or a house in the late 1700s. Did Caroline want to marry me because I was the last surviving Ravenglass? How did she uncover the truth when others couldn't? The land alone would be—my god, if only I had known that the Ravenglass owned the land and the house Wendy wanted us to buy. She'd been right about renting the land and water frontage out. If I could prove my claim to being the last surviving member of the family the property would automatically be mine. We would then have money to spend on the house. The estate agent's details said the building was over two hundred years old.

Caroline's sharp tone brought me back to my senses. "Yes, we are related, but that does not stop us from marrying."

"I get your point as distant cousins we can, but not first cousins. So that's why the brother couldn't end the bet, by just joining the families and allowing their children to marry." I patted her hand gently, hoping to encourage her to say more. Once her charade was over, with the new information, I could claim ownership. Caroline turned away, but not before, I saw a morbid flicker of pleasure in her narrowing eyes. "Caroline—I—" I muttered, trying to find the right words. When she turned back, her mood had lifted as her eyes shone brightly on meeting mine.

"The house is almost ready for us," she said, tugging at my hand. "Once we set our wedding day, the rest of the furniture will be moved in. Blake, it will be so wonderful after all these years of waiting to be your wife, Mrs Blake Ravenglass. Let no one put asunder, not even in death."

As we climbed the stone steps to the raised patio, I grasped my shoulder as an agonising pain made me drop to my knees.

"My love, are you alright?"

I tried to focus on Caroline's face. What was the witch doing to me? My mind filled with millions of speeded-up images that raced through my head. My stomach heaved at the sight of a child struggling in the water, fighting for his life, followed by a bright light, and then Reg and Dora appearing and fading into a party, a forgotten girl, Wendy's smiling face, my beautiful daughters, and then an all-consuming fire followed by nothing. A voice screamed words I didn't understand then darkness fell.

The next moment, I stood in a study with my hand pressed against a windowpane taking in the view across the estuary. The sun was high in the clear-blue summer sky while swifts and swallows raced along the water's edge, their amazing twists and turns amused me. The fields of golden corn were swaying gently. I was happy and contented in a highly decorative room surrounded by bookshelves full of leather-bound books. Behind was an oak desk, and a red leather sofa and two matching armchairs were placed before an ornate marble fireplace. The click of a door opening made me turn. My heart raced at the sight of the woman who had entered the study. "Oh, my darling, you look stunning, Wendy," I said as I took her in my arms.

"Blake, this house is amazing. You said you would build me a beautiful home to raise our children in. I cannot wait to meet your family."

"I'm so pleased you love it as much as I do, Wendy. Now we are married it's our forever home."

"What about your cousin? Your mother said she wasn't happy about the news you had taken a wife."

"Caroline was already married when I asked you to be my wife. She does not have the same temperament as you, my darling. You, my dearest, are sweet and kind. And, so too will our children. She was never going to be my choice for a wife. Forget about her, she can't do anything to us, darling Wendy."

CHAPTER FIFTEEN

"Come back, Blake, you promised me we would be married." A harsh and bitter voice called me away.

"Marry you! Why are you doing this to me? I had never met you before until we worked together. Now you tell me we are cousins."

"Yes, we are cousins and grew up together in our own time. The house is punishing you for your betrayal. You must remember the promise we made to each other?" She smiled, but something deep within her eyes revealed such cruelty. "We made a promise to each other years ago that nothing would keep us apart? But you escaped into the future leaving me trapped. I found a way to follow you. Now the house has brought you back to me again."

Now I understood the house had been trying to warn me about its link to my past. I knew for sure Caroline was dangerous and chose my words carefully. This landscape linked both Caroline and me. I met her gaze with a reassuring smile and said, "We played here as children dreaming our dreams."

"Oh, Blake you do remember." Her excitement shone. "We were going to build our castle here." She spun around in front of the house. Her dress became a wave of shimmering blue and white petticoats. I caught sight of her slender ankles just before she came to an abrupt halt. With piercing fiery eyes, she said, "You promised me you would fight dragons for me. I, your queen forever, and then you went away to fight in a foreign land and nearly died."

"Caroline, we were children, dreaming childish dreams. I had to surrender my childhood, and become a man to fight for my country."

"You did not have to go to war."

"What would your father have thought of me then? In his eyes, I wouldn't have been a suitable husband for his daughter."

"What about the promise you made to me, Blake? With you away, Papa had me marry for wealth. He cared nothing for my feelings, but I made sure it would never last, while I waited for your return."

"What are you saying?"

She laughed. "Papa hates educated women. So, I educated myself. It was easy to find the answer from an old Grimoire book in his library. It was too easy really," she said with a devilish glint in her eyes. "Once I knew what I needed to know, it changed everything. Papa has his fortune. We were married only in name. I did not allow that man to lay a hand on me. I gave him a little something to help ease him from a light sleep to a deeper one. They laughed and said the excitement was too much. Of course, his children were not happy as I inherited everything. Come; let me show you the inside of the house. I have the key." Caroline pulled a large key from a tiny cloth bag she carried. "I made Papa promise me, he would bring you home. After Archie died, it was easier for me to get whatever I wanted."

"How did your brother die?"

"A weak heart, the doctor said, though I might have helped him along a little bit." She laughed and she pushed open the door.

I followed Caroline in, knowing the visions had revealed the truth, but Caroline's revelations made me nervous. Had the woman murdered twice? The hallway was spacious, with a sweeping ornate staircase. Not long ago, Wendy and I climbed it carefully, avoiding areas riddled with dry rot and woodworm. Caroline chatted about her father hiring servants for us as I followed on. My hand caressed the familiar banister feeling the knots in the wood. On the landing before us, Caroline opened a door and stood back. I stepped in. The view was amazing. In my time, Wendy had spun around in the sunbeam and dust in the dirty dark room. Over two hundred years ago, it had been a light, bright space. "It's a study," I said as I took in the red leather suite, the marble fireplace, and empty bookshelves. "My study."

"Yes, only the best for my husband."

"But—"

"Yes, Blake—" Her voice was light but edged blood red.

I walked over to the window and looked out. I realised I had built the house, not Caroline's father. The house was to have been my forever home with Wendy of the past and the Wendy of the future at my side, but somehow Caroline had robbed me of my home, identity, and life. The pain in my shoulder throbbed as I turned to face her.

She smiled, took hold of my hand, and pulled me towards the door, "Come my love, let me show you the rest of our home."

*

Finally, we arrived back in the kitchen. Caroline's excitement filled the large room as she chatted about the maids and kitchen staff we would need. I wasn't listening but thinking of a way to stop all the craziness. Copper pots shone on shelves while an old-style cooking range filled one side of the room. Under a window was a double sink with what looked to be a hand pump. At the centre stood a large scrubbed pine table, while against the other wall was a pine dresser that almost groaned under the weight of what seemed to be bottled fruits, vegetables, and preserves. China bowls and dishes stood ready for a cook to arrive.

I pulled my arm free from hers and staggered backwards. "I don't know what you have done to me, but I can't marry you."

"But you will this time. You'll never be free from me; I will hunt you down throughout time until we are married."

"You're mad!"

"Am I, Blake." A wry smile crossed her lips as her eyes darkened. "I've made sure I've destroyed your future and past. I have the power to continue hunting you forever until you marry me freely. You and Wendy will never ever find happiness together. You promise to make me your queen. This house will be my castle. Not some labourer's daughter who nursed you in a hospital miles away." The wildness in her eyes faded, reminding me of my indiscretion that afternoon in the car.

Of course, my only escape was the wall. If it worked the first time, I reasoned it would happen again and made contact with the wall behind me. Once again, the bricks began to absorb me. Caroline's laughter was inaudible to me now. All I could hear was a whooshing sound that echoed like bells clanging in some distant time or space.

CHAPTER SIXTEEN

On opening my eyes, I saw, through an opaque film, a shape moving within a dark, neglected room. A familiar voice was calling to me.

"Blake, where are you?"

I tried to move, to call out, but the sound wouldn't come. A light flashed, and for a moment, I could see more than a blur. Wendy stood holding a phone.

"Oh, dear gods, I'm so sorry, Blake for blaming you for what happened to our girls. I'm the one to blame. I betrayed us all by putting my wants before yours and our children. Motherhood had sucked me dry and I wanted to be myself again," she sobbed. "The internet made it too easy to give into weakness, to see your inadequacies. If only I hadn't met Caroline online. I just wanted someone I could talk to and she was there. I should've spoken to Maggie, but I didn't think she would understand, not having children herself. Then one day, Caroline said we should meet. Maggie loved having the children. It became so easy to lie, had an appointment, or needed to buy something special for you or the children. Maggie said she understood it was easier to shop without the children. It was exciting, planning our little get-togethers. I felt alive. Carefully chose what to wear rather than smelling of nappies and baby sick. It wasn't as though I was being unfaithful to you, Blake."

I couldn't believe we had both been such fools. I wanted to take Wendy in my arms and tell her I forgave her, but the more I struggled to free myself, the tighter my chest became and the harder it was to breathe.

Wendy went on.

"She was so glamorous. When she walked into a room, the place lit up. All eyes turned to her. I wanted to be her. For months, I wanted to tell you, I was leaving. Caroline said she could show me the world, and I believed her. Oh, Blake, why couldn't I see it was all make-believe, some stupid fantasy to destroy our happiness?

The plan was I was supposed to meet up with her, but I panicked when she arrived at the house. You hadn't arrived home yet. Just before the fire started, she followed me indoors and yelled, telling me terrible things about you."

Bloody Caroline had been to my house. I struggled, making it hard to breathe.

Wendy continued with her confession. "She said you had always loved her. Your destiny was to be together with her. She used me to get to you I didn't believe her when she said she could prove it. This house was yours and hers. Anyway, on the day of the fire, I went to the car to bring my things in and tried texting you to warn you to hurry home because she wouldn't leave the house. That's when the fire started. I don't know how. I keep playing it over in my mind. I messed up and blamed you. Caroline had disappeared, and there was no sign of her on the net. I have no proof; she started the fire, just my word against hers. The children are gone, and now I've lost you too, Blake. You were right about not coming here, but I wanted to see the house for myself, maybe it's my destiny to die here with you."

Powerless to do anything, but watch, trapped within the wall, I saw Wendy raise something to her lips. A bottle. She tipped her head back and gave an agonising cough as the bottle smashed on the floor.

"I will always love you, Blake."

Wendy touched the wall behind her. And I wondered if she knew I was trapped there. By the light of her phone, I saw torment mark her features before it fell from her hand as she slid down the wall. Her back arched for a few seconds before she slumped forward. The phone died; I closed my eyes as the darkness fell.

Suddenly I was floating, unsure whether it was air or water. A strangeness encased my body as images ran backwards in my mind, gathering speed until thunder roared in my ears until I couldn't breathe. Panic took hold as I tried to struggle towards a blinding light. Waves of gurgling bubbles rose around me, popping against my skin and in my hair. I shook with cold. I realised I could hear a muffled sound and focused on it until it cleared and became a voice and then words.

"You're all right, lad. You're safe now."

Arms gripped me under my armpits, digging into my flesh. They felt warm against my skin as I became aware of a shimmering blue light. Then with an explosion, the blue light became a white light that roared with hundreds of different noises until slowly I recognised them individually; the sound of birds, insects, and traffic. A reassuring voice said, "We'll soon have you dry and warm." A stiff cloth rubbed at my hair, arms, back, and legs. "What's your name, boy?"

"Ravenglass, I'm Ravenglass!" I said.

This time I will rewrite my destiny and take back the house from Caroline forever...

BIOGRAPHY

Paula R. C. Readman is married with one son, Stewart. She was born in Essex and raised next to an ancient watermill, but her heart belongs in the Yorkshire land of her ancestors. Paula started writing late in life after setting herself a challenge to see if she could get something in print before her next big birthday. She has more than exceeded her expectations since English Heritage published her first short story in 2010. Paula has now had over a hundred short stories published, five books, and has won several writing competitions, including the Harrogate Crime Writing Festival/Writing Magazine short story competition in 2012. In February 2020, DEMAIN Publishing published *The Funeral Birds* the first of five books published over the course of the last four years.

Stone Angels published by Darkstroke
Seeking the Dark published by Darkstroke
The Phoenix Hour published by Darkstroke
Days Pass like Shadow published by Bridge House Publishing
Never Reaching the End published by DEMAIN Publishing.

For more information about Paula and her writing visit:

Facebook:
https://facebook.com/paula.readman.1

Twitter: Paula R C Readman@Darkfantasy13

Or just Google, Paula R. C. Readman, and you'll find her.

DEMAIN PUBLISHING

To keep up to-date on all news DEMAIN (including future submission calls and releases) you can follow us in a number of ways:

BLOG:
www.demainpublishingblog.weebly.com

TWITTER:
@DemainPubUk

FACEBOOK PAGE:
Demain Publishing

INSTAGRAM:
demainpublishing

Printed in Poland
by Amazon Fulfillment
Poland Sp. z o.o., Wrocław

23764915R00063